Cornucopia

Poems by Bridget Renshaw

In memory of my grandmother,

Little Mama.

The Ferris Wheel

"Mom! I want to ride the Ferris Wheel!"
"What? Have you lost your head?"

Then up, up, up so high, I think I almost touched the sky.
Then down, down, down below, to wave 'Hi' and 'Hello'.
I wave without a doubt, to the people who had chickened out.

Then round, round, round so quick.
Uhhh, I think I'm getting sick!

The Feels

Feels go in and feels go out.
They keep you warm while they swarm about.

They can come on so quick,
And sometimes they stick.

They keep you calm. They get you stirred.
They keep you clear. They make your visions blurred.

They feel like goose bumps inside of you.
There are different kinds and you can choose.

They may weaken you, but can make you strong.
The feels, those feels, come through like a song.

Breakables

I don't like being in stores with breakables.
I'm afraid that I'm going to break everything.
They always have those "don't touch" labels.
I'm afraid I may shatter something with my arm swing.

What if I turn a little to the side?
Will my backpack knock over the glass?
I'm trying to have a real slow stride,
So I can make a really clean pass.

I can't relax in a store like that.
I walk around with my arms at my side.
I can barely even have a chat.
I'll just wait for you outside.

Scattered Thoughts

What time is it? I'm getting hungry.
What's that smell? I think my socks smell funky.

Seriously, tummy, you need to calm down.
My tummy gets a lil grumpy, probably has a frown.

My stomach sounds like my grandma when she's muttering.
That cloud looks like a butterfly fluttering.

I wish I could be a butterfly for a day.
I'd fly up, up, up and away.

But I mean, of course I'd come back down here.
I wonder how high things can fly when the weather is clear.

I like the rain. I like the weather when it rains.
And the smell of rain, smells like a metal chain.

I haven't ridden my bike in a while.
I wonder if I could go a mile.
I wonder what makes everyone smile.

I smile when I'm laughing, but other times too.
I'll think of something from the past and smile out of the blue.

Out of the blue, I wonder what that means.
Come to think of it, I wonder about a lot of things.

Is that just me, or does everyone wonder their way through the day?
I wonder about the wonders people wonder when they're wondering away.

I think it's cool we can think about anything we want in our head.
It's private stuff, it's important, you heard what I said.

Is that a quarter on the ground? Oh, no it's just trash.
Pick up your trash people, is that too much to ask?

I don't like asking questions, I just use clues to figure things out.
What's that noise loudly rumbling about?

Oh yeah! I'm hungry and I need to eat.
Look at all the lines on my hand, isn't that neat?

Kelly the Kitten's Rough Day

Kelly the kitten had a rough day.

She sat by a rock when she went out to play.

She was startled when the rock started moving.

It wasn't a rock at all that she was viewing.

She went back inside as fast as she could.

What happened out there was not very good.

When I Grow Up

"I don't know what I want to be when I grow up," is what I told Mrs. Sweetberry.
She said, "Well, do you want to be a teacher?" I thought, "Quite the contrary".

I said, "Mrs. Sweetberry, I don't know what I want to be right now, maybe it doesn't exist".
She said, "Just write down a normal job that you think you might like, right here on this list".

I said, "Mrs. Sweetberry, I don't know what I want to be, but I'll figure it out later".
She said, "Well for now just write down any job right here on this piece of paper".

I said, "Mrs. Sweetberry, once I learn what I'm good at and enjoy, then I'll create something new".
She said, "Okay sweetheart, but for right now you must finish this project, it is due".

I sat there with a pen and paper and thought about it as much as I could.
I didn't know what I would be right this instant, but I knew I eventually would.

I picked up my pen and I scribbled really fast.
I put the paper on her desk and shuffled out of class.

I looked back and saw her read it. She looked surprised but pleased.
I wrote when I grow up, I hope I can be the best possible me I can be.

Mom's Clever Little Trick

My Mom got brilliant yesterday when I was being obnoxious.
Don't tell her I told you this, because her plan was pretty flawless.

I was dancing around, making a mess, and singing.
I told her I was bored and she needed to entertain me.

She said, "Ok, why don't we play hide and seek?"
That's my favorite game so I said, "Ok, don't peek!"

I ran fast as she counted, I had a new hiding place.
I got in the bathroom in a little bitty space.

I could hear her say things like, "Man! I can't find Lucas anywhere!"
And, "Nope he's not in the closet and not under the chair."

I couldn't help but giggle. I tried to do it quietly.
I had obviously chosen my hiding spot wisely.

After a little while, it was getting kind of cramped.
I could probably come out now, I was obviously the champ.

I snuck out and then I saw what my Mom was doing.
She was just sitting on the couch, she wasn't even looking!

She tricked me, my tricky little Mother.
I'm going to use that trick on my brother.

How I Slept?

My teacher asked me how I slept last night.

I thought, "Does she not know how?"

I wasn't sure if I was wrong or right,

But I said, "I just closed my eyes and laid down."

Risks

Jenny didn't like risks. They weren't her thing.

She just liked what a very normal day would bring.

She never really liked to try anything new.

For Jenny, she just didn't do things out of the blue.

She enjoyed a normal day without any predicaments.

She didn't like when things were different.

For years and years she lived a life of balance,

And after 80 years of life, nothing much has happened.

Technology

Technology is fun.
Technology is neat.
Technology makes it easy
To get what I need.

It brings the far, nearer.
It is everywhere I go.
It makes the world clearer.
It teaches me what I should know.
I bring it along everywhere I go.

I look up facts and things that are fun.
I play lots of games until my batteries are done.
I watch the real world as it passes me by.
The world seems unfulfilling, but I'm not sure why.

As I started getting older and my days drifted away,
I decided to go out and look at the day.
There was nobody out there with whom I could play.
"They're busy with me," Technology waved.
"I've got all of their sunny days saved."

My Astronaut Days

Sometimes, I pretend I'm an astronaut.
I put underwear on my head and look out the leg slot.

I walk around like there is no gravity.
I walk on the couch until my Mom gets mad at me.

I have a lot of astronaut conversations.
I tell my Mom we should go to Mars for vacation.

I pretend that Cuddles is a little alien cat.
Cuddles is NOT okay with that.

Squirt the Squirrel

Squirt the squirrel was hungry.

It was the afternoon on Monday.

He went to the park for some air.

He had some wind-blown hair.

He saw a bag so he took a looksy.

Inside the bag was a sugar cookie!

He carried it up, up, up the tree.

On Monday squirt was pretty happy.

Jenny Non-Stop

They called her Jenny Non-Stop.

She was a hippo who loved to dance hip-hop!

Sometimes her Mom would tell her to chill.

Jenny couldn't help it, she never sat still.

She grooved at home, down the streets and in the halls at school.

For a challenge she'd hip-hop on a hippo sized stool.

She's a little more careful now because of last week.

She shook the streets a little bit with her dancing feet.

The people just laughed, they loved Jenny Non-Stop.

She was trying out her new move that she called the drop-hop.

Board-Game-Aggressive

It's hard for me to play board games.
I get way too competitive.
I have winning running through my veins,
And sometimes I get board-game-aggressive.

I know it's just a game with friends,
But I want to win so badly.
I say I don't care about winning, but that's pretend,
Winning is what I want exactly.

I'm having a game night with my friend Joe,
So here I am, playing and smiling.
My smile is real this time, though.
I'm winning all the games and it's exciting!

I better calm down a little bit,
So Joe will want to play games with me again.

Chug the Slug

Chug the slug needed a lift.

He had something important to do.

He needed to get somewhere quick.

He needed to call someone and he knew who.

He called his friend Speedy.

Speedy said he would be there soon.

Chug felt a little needy.

Speedy got there in an hour, around noon.

He told Chug to hop on.

He would get him there in a jiffy.

They got there before dawn.

Isn't that nifty?

I Wanted to Make a Cake

I wanted to make a cake.
I asked my Mom to tell me the recipe.
She seemed pleased I wanted to bake,
So she began to tell me splendidly.

She said first you take all of the ingredients,
Then you mix, stir and beat. I pulled up a chair.
It started to seem pretty tedious,
So I said, "Let me stop you right there."

My Mom's Friend, Susan

My Mom had a tea party and invited her friend Susan.
Susan was nice and all, but I couldn't get passed my confusion.

She kept talking and talking, and she would drink her tea.
That's not what I would be doing, if that were me.

Susan talked about her kids and the vacation they were about to take,
But all I could think was, "Is she going to eat her cupcake?"

Inner Pilot

She was kind of quiet.

She kept to herself.

In her mind she was a pilot.

Flying somewhere else.

Flying fast.

Going places.

Far and vast.

Open spaces.

An aspiring pond.

A creative key.

She thought beyond

What she could see.

Umbrella-Free

Sally didn't carry an umbrella.
She liked to feel the rain.
She didn't want to treat it like a dilemma.
She was happy when it came.

Homework?!

Homework? Homework! No I can't!

After school, I had a different plan.

I was maybe going to ride my bike.

Maybe I would even go on a nature hike.

I could learn about the world around me,

I could read a book or climb a tree.

If I didn't have homework, I could write the next hit song.

I could learn to play my guitar if I could practice all night long.

I could figure out a way to solve the world's problems.

The world would cheer for me saying, "You're so awesome!"

It's just not fair, all this work after school hours.

I just wish I had super powers!

I would send a message to my teacher's brain,

That homework is mean and is such a strain.

Kids need to have fun after a long day of school,

And giving them homework is just not cool.

If I have to do this homework, I'm going to scream and cry.

It hurts my soul to do homework, why, oh why?

Then, in a sweet tone, I heard Mrs. Carnahan say,

"Your homework is to have some fun today!"

Oh, Mrs. Carnahan, you're the very, very best!

I no longer have to be so stressed.

My Mom drove me home with my good spirit restored.

"Mom, what is there to do today? I'm sooo bored!!"

Mom's Little Helper

Not to brag or anything, but I'm my Mom's little helper.
I love it when she flashes me a smile like I'm the greatest child ever.
You name it, I'm here for you Mom, just keep giving me all those compliments.
Like when you say I'm just the best, you know, those kinds of comments.
Don't sweat it, for a child like me, it's all in a day's work.
For having such a great kid, it's just one of your millions of perks.
The kitchen? I cleaned it. The trash? Already took it out.
Did I clean my room? Mom, without a doubt.
So now I'm just going to kick my feet up and wait for my Mom to walk in.
When she excitedly says, "Wow, who cleaned?" I'll turn red and grin.
Then I'll run into the kitchen and say, "Mom, it was me!"
She'll say I'm the best little helper and I'm afraid I'll have to agree.

Nervous Anticipation

I'm sitting here and I'm sweating, my heart is beating so fast.
I have to tap my foot on the ground until this all has passed.
The second hand on the clock could not possibly tick any slower.
I'm trying to sink down in my chair, but I don't think I can go any lower.
Avoid eye contact, yes, that is what I'll do,
Oh look at all the dust on the floor, yup just lookin' at my shoe.
I'll just think about something else until this time goes by.
I wonder what I'll eat for dinner, I just hope there's pie.
Yeah there it is, I'm starting to get really hot.
Maybe I'll just run out of here, now there's a thought!
But then I'd probably have to explain and I'm not sure what I'd say.
EW what is that on my shoe, did I step in something gray?
And then I heard it, finally, I was getting worried about my health.
My teacher called on somebody for an answer but she called on somebody else.

Be Unique

This is a little story about a girl named Marley.
Her mom was a school teacher, and her dad drove a Harley.

She wore glasses, headbands, and she spoke with a squeak.
The kids called her weird, but she liked being unique.

She had wild crazy curls that spun into the air.
She had a friendly smile and lots and lots of hair.

She was quirky, funny, and one of a kind.
She had lots of positivity swimming through her mind.

When she walked through school, all the kids stared.
They said she was bizarre, but Marley never cared.

What was really bizarre, is those kids that pointed out her flaws,
Really just wanted to be unique and different, just like Marley was.

Weekend Pick-Me-Ups

On Friday and Saturday nights, I get to stay up real late.
I watch movies on the couch for as long I can stay awake.

Between the TV and handfuls of popcorn, I usually doze off.
My dad usually does too, because I can hear him snore and cough.

Then I can hear my mom wake up my dad and start to speak real softly.
They are discussing if they should carry me to bed so I lay real calmly.

I could get up and walk to bed, but I'm really, really sleepy.
So if there are talks about carrying me that would make it really easy.

It is usually my dad who comes over and gets me.
He carries me to bed while I pretend that I'm still sleeping.

Weekend nights are the best, because I just need to relax.
I need a nighttime pick-me-up after a long week of class.

Cooper Was Embarrassed

Cooper was embarrassed.
He did something awkward.
However, in all fairness,
He was tired from last night's soccer.

He went up to his teacher.
He had a simple question.
It was the normal procedure
For an inquiry on the lesson.

He was confused on number four,
And so was his friend Tom.
But instead of calling his teacher Mrs. Moore,
He accidently called her Mom.

Syd the Skunk under the Elephant's Trunk

A friendly guy he was, Syd the skunk.
He sat all day by Ed the Elephant's trunk.
Wherever Ed went, Syd would be there.
He liked to follow under Ed's trunk everywhere!
Then one day he started walking to the side of Ed.
He said that it was better for his head.
Because yesterday there was a pollen-filled breeze,
And all over Syd, Ed let out a huge sneeze.

Lost Balloon

I let go of my balloon and it took off.
I really liked that balloon a lot!

I watched it soar into the sky and then I lost sight.
I hope my little balloon is doing alright.

I put up signs all over the neighborhood.
If you have seen it, let me know if you could.

Maybe it was time my balloon was set free.
It had seemed a bit antsy that day to me.

Maybe it was time the balloon went out on its own.
That time in every balloon's life when it discovers the unknown.

This Way

I go this way,
Most of the time.
That area is gray,
And there's a mountain to climb.

After some years,
I wonder what might have happened.
If I fought through my fears,
And climbed over that mountain.

Choices come.
Choices go.
You are where you're from.
You don't really know.

I think I might,
From now on,
Put up a fight,
Before the years are gone.

WHO?

I THOUGHT THE OWL OUTSIDE WAS NEAT.

I THOUGHT HE COULD TEACH ME SOME LESSONS.

HE SAID, "WHO? WHO?" I SAID, "ME."

I WISH HE DIDN'T ASK SO MANY QUESTIONS.

Selling Happiness

If I could sell happiness I would.

I would sell it to everyone I could.

I'd trade it for their sadness and tears.

I'd give them hope in exchange for their fears.

I would open up a shop and put in a drive-thru.

Here are some good feelings for you and you and you.

Do you need a smile? Here are five.

You'll feel so happy to be alive.

You'll leave with a grin that's as big as your face.

You'll want to keep coming back to this place.

If you have any rotten feelings, you gotta leave those behind.

That's the cost of the good things, because they are one of a kind.

If I Never Slept

If I never went to sleep, I would get so much done.
I would do my homework and chores before I saw the sun.

Then I'd have all this free time during the sunshine of the day.
Those pesky tasks would be done and I would go out and play.

I have always wondered what happens at night all around me.
I would get to see what happens at night when I sleep.

If there really are monsters in my closet, I would certainly find out.
They wouldn't be the only ones at night out and about.

I would sit and watch some TV with all my extra time.
I'd kick my feet up and relax from the daily grind.

I'm trying so hard to stay awake. I'm putting up a fight.
Oh no, I definitely need to sleep now, I wish th....... Goodnight.

Fishing Days

Here I am, fishing with grandpa,
Not catching anything at all.

Listening to all of his stories,
About all the big fish he has caught and all the glory.

I never catch anything when I fish with grandpa.
I never catch anything at all.

Sometimes I tiptoe.

Sometimes I whisper.

Under the wind flow,

I'm a drifter.

I'm not too sure,

What leads me where.

There is no cure.

My adventure affair.

I'll be right back.

I'll see you soon.

An escapade I lack,

And it's playing my tune.

I may be here.

I may be there.

I'll always be near.

I'm just not sure where.

The Bubble in My Bath

I probably won't ever forget it.
It was weird and just not right.
I took a bath with bubbles for a bit,
Before I went to bed for the night.

I was splashing and playing.
Bubble baths were my favorite.
All the rubber duckies were swaying.
Even the ducks had smiling faces.

Then, how it happened, who knows?
It was just so unexpected.
One of the bubbles came out of…my nose,
And I just felt so affected.

I sat there for a second, puzzled.
I didn't, but I wanted to cry.
What a sneaky little bubble.
How did it get inside?

Clowning Chloe

Clowning Chloe was pretty lucky.

She got to ride in the grocery buggy.

She had fun, and even though it was quirky,

Chloe did this until she was 30.

I Named My Puppy Grandpa

I got a new puppy. I named him Grandpa.
I take lots of pictures of him with my camera.

I picked his name because I thought it was funny.
Like when I say, "Grandpa, stop being so grumpy!"

I always run over to him and pet him on his tummy.
I say, "Do you want a treat, Grandpa? It's so yummy."

"Who's a good boy?" I ask. Then I say, "YOU ARE!"
I say that when he fetches the ball that I threw really far.

"Grandpa, get down," I say when he climbs on things.
He doesn't really walk yet, he just waddles and springs.

What a silly dog. He's everything I've always wanted.
And yesterday, just like an old grandpa, he grunted.

Don't Be the Timid Squirrel

Don't be the squirrel that gets stuck in the middle.
The one that stands in the street, timid and fickle.
Make a decision, and make things happen.
You don't want to be the squirrel that gets flattened.

This Little Banana

This little guy, I wonder what happened.

Somebody was up to some funny business I imagine.

I went to the store for a Sunday extravaganza.

Then I saw something happened to this sweet little banana.

I looked at it and saw that the little guy was bruised.

I looked around and then whispered to it, "who did this to you?"

Finn's Squeaky Cart

Finn got the squeaky cart at the store.

It was pesky and loud, I must mention.

The squeaks made him like it more.

Everyone stared, but he liked the attention.

Penguin Dreamin'

Jed was a penguin who wanted to fly.
"I have wings and determination, oh why can't I?"

"I see all of these birds, flappin' around over the sea.
Why oh why can that not be me?"

He would waddle around and flap as hard as he could.
Why he would jump, flap and then land back on the ice, he never quite understood.

"Maybe tomorrow," he'd say with purpose.
"If I get this down, I'm joining the circus."

On and on and on he went.
It became quite the daily event.

And once, just once, he kind of flew.
"I did it, just a little, now I need something else to do!"

Molly and Boris

Each day, Molly and Boris,

Were up on their high horses.

They were soul mates and full of love

But never came down from up above.

They went separate ways, Molly and Boris.

Atop their high, high horses.

My Grandpa Doesn't Like Change

My Grandpa, boy does he hate change.
You give him toast for breakfast and he thinks you're so strange.

He has waffles and coffee every morning and usually chicken every night.
If you try something different, he'll put up a great big fight.

He still reads the newspaper and doesn't like the computer and things.
He watches the same television station and only the shows that station brings.

He thinks everything I do is silly and talks about life back in his day.
They don't sound that great, the games he used to play.

But he's my Grandpa and I love him, so I'll just do what he wants.
Except for tomorrow morning, I'm replacing his waffles with croissants.

Alien Waiting

Every night between 6:50 and 8,
I sit in my chair outside and I wait.

I wait to see if there are any aliens hanging around.
I'd like to be the one they take from the ground.

I think my baby brother looks like an alien, maybe.
At least he did when he was a baby.

Just letting you know my rationality.
Aliens, I'm ready to go if you'll have me.
I have a really great personality.

SHE STRAIGHTENED, SHE STRAIGHTENED

She fixed the clocks and straightened the frames.
She knew everyone by their full names.

It was a little off, so she straightened the chair.
She always, only, puts one foot on each stair.

She fixed the clocks again because they were a little off.
She straightened the frames again, just because.

She got up to straighten a picture and got up again to change it back.
She straightened up my bookshelf because it was out of whack.

To get her to sit down, you had to put up a fight.
They told her to relax, but she didn't know what that was like.

Hey, You're Okay

Hey, you're okay.

Don't let the day get away.

It's just a little issue.

Don't get out the tissues.

Don't be cheerless,

It's not that serious.

Let it go without delay.

I promise you'll be okay.

Laugh It Out

I finally figured out what it means to really laugh it out.

When you laugh, you see, you shake all of the grumpiness about.

It breaks it up into the tiniest little pieces.

Then it evaporates right out of you and your happiness increases!

It sounds really crazy but I can guarantee it's true.

Because the other day at Grandma's, at about one or two,

I was grumpy, angry and just really mad at the day.

Then Grandma said something funny, so I laughed and began to shake.

I rolled around and around for a while on the floor.

Then when I stopped laughing, I forgot what I was mad about before.

Sara Spreet

Sara Spreet was way too neat.
She always had matching socks on her feet.

Everything in her room was where it should go,
From her tidy, tidy toy box, to her shoes in a neat, neat row.

Her bed was so clean, it looked like nobody slept there.
There was not a mess or a thing out of place anywhere.

Sara Spreet was way too neat.
Sara loved to organize and she was oh so sweet.

Her friend Timmy said it had gone too far already,
When he noticed Sara Spreet organizing her spaghetti.

Refrigerator of Success

Whenever we do something great,
Mom puts it up on the refrigerator.
It's an easy place to portray,
Our great work for everyone to see later.

I've done a lot of great things lately,
And I wanted everyone to know.
It might look a little bit crazy,
But I put them all up there for show.

I made a bracelet, I was proud of that.
I was proud of finishing my dinner plate.
I put that up there by my cool new hat.
I can tie my shoes now, so they needed a place.

Perhaps I got a little carried away.
Because when my Dad came home later,
He was looking for his yogurt parfait,
But couldn't find the refrigerator!

Dance Party

I was home by myself and danced like no one was watching.
I was spinning, swirling and my feet were criss-crossing.

I was about as free as a bird, and feeling mighty fine.
I danced around everywhere, like a star who was ready to shine.

I was rocking out about hard as possible.
The music was up and the furniture was no obstacle.

I spun around and danced with my cat Lola.
I didn't care who saw me, I did ballet on the sofa!

"I'll dance in front of the world," I thought, as I put on my ballet costume.
Then my parents walked in, so I ran quickly to my room.

My Fort

I built a fort in my room, as you can clearly see.
I got some big sheets and pinned them up, looks pretty good to me.

My Mom was all like, "Can I come inside? Pretty please?"
I said, "Mom, of course! This place is for everyone, no fees."

I think I'll call it my Everyone-Fort, because anyone can chill in here.
Big, small, short, tall, cats, dogs, and even you if you bring some cheer.

This is a place where everyone is welcome to come hang out.
It's going to be suuuper fun and I can say that without a doubt!

If somebody can't find just the right place they belong,
There's room in this here fort and we all get along!

Everyone get over here, it's a place we can all be.
There's room for you, and of course, there's room for me.

When Freddy Threw Me a Beat

I wanted to be a rapper. All I needed was a beat.

So I asked my friend Freddy who always tapped his feet.

He said, "Yeah I'm not doing anything, I can throw you beats today".

Freddy was really good and he threw me beats all day.

I said, "Give me a good one Freddy, I've got something good".

Then he gave me a beat better than I ever thought he could.

I said, I said....

"Yo, yo yo, I'm Bradley and I'm neat.

I wear cool shoes everyday on my feet.

Walkin' around, I dance to my own beat,

With a little help from Freddy, before he goes home to eat.

Yo I've got a little story,

Bout my life all day, today.

I think I'll follow my glory,

Instead of going out to play.

You see I wanna be a rapper.

I'm cool calm and dapper.

There will be lots of clappers,

When I show up with my swagger.

I hope you all are ready,

And yes I'm bringing Freddy."

EXCLAMATION MARKS!

I LOVE TO USE EXCLAMATION MARKS!

THEY GET A LOT OF ATTENTION!!

I USE THEM AFTER EVERY REMARK!!!

I EVEN USE THEM WHEN I HAVE A QUESTION!!!!

Rough Week at Grandma's

Whenever I go to Grandma's, life gets a little rough.
I have to do things for myself, and sometimes it gets tough.

Sometimes I don't brush my hair or just skip my shower,
Because grandma doesn't notice and it takes like an hour.

I play around all day, inside and out.
I sure get dirty and messy as I wonder all about.

Grandma doesn't care, and she cooks us a big dinner.
I feel like in the contest of grandmas, mine is the winner!

She says we don't have to brush our teeth if we eat an apple instead.
I know that's not the truth, but I eat an apple before bed.

One thing that we don't go without,
Is all the love she throws about.

So even when I come back home and I look like quite a mess,
When I spend a week at grandmas, I feel truly blessed!

Watson Looked Sharp

Franny liked to dress up Watson, her wiener dog,
In suits, hats, ties, and things like that.
He had the cutest outfits when he was on the jog.
His favorite was his coat and top hat.

People said dogs don't like to wear clothes,
But they really didn't know Watson.
He enjoyed looking sharp and striking a pose.
After all, there could be some cute dogs watching.

My Baby Brother

My baby brother is way too adorable.
He gets all the attention and it's horrible.

His face looks like precious and cute had a kid together,
And they've bundled the rest of him up for this cold weather!

The kid looks like a squishy marshmallow with a face.
I'm over it, and I'm going to get my own place.

He's not even...oh...oh my...he just smiled.
I love him forever. I think I'll stay here awhile.

My Birthday Cake

I wanted to eat my birthday cake, I did.

I love chocolate cake and I'm a hungry kid.

Plus it was my birthday, so I was feeling special.

It's just that it was starting to get so stressful.

It was almost time to eat that big cake I desired,

So why oh why did my Mom set it on fire?

Fletcher Never Shared

Fletcher, young Fletcher, he never shared.

He never shared and he didn't care.

What's his, is his, and nobody else's.

To sum it all up, Fletcher was selfish.

One day in class he needed a piece of paper,

But nobody wanted to do him a favor.

When Somebody Says Your Name

My parents had friends over, so I made the decision,

To play in my room instead of the kitchen.

I couldn't hear what my parents were saying.

I didn't care, I was too busy playing.

I couldn't hear my parents' friends either.

I was in my room taking a breather.

Something stuck out all of the sudden,

From downstairs mid-discussion,

They abruptly had all of my attention.

I heard my name and I needed to listen.

The Automatic Sink Match

Hey sink, I'm right here.
I'm ready for water to come out.
I've already got soap everywhere,
And I'm moving my hands all about.

Maybe if I talk to you nicely,
Hey sink, you're so pretty.
I'm sure you have a great personality.
Can we please do this quickly?

Maybe if I'm stern with you.
Hey sink, come on hurry it up.
I've got to get to class,
and I've had about enough.

Maybe if I walk away and walk back.
I'll pretend I'm someone new.
Well hello there sink,
I'm Alfred from England, how do you do?

Sink! are you serious?
Stop being so rotten.
Do you know how to work or have you forgotten?

I'll just sit here and wait,
Until you do what you do.
Just whenever you're ready,
My hands will be here for you.

Having a "Me" Night

Tonight I'm having a "me" night.
No friends and definitely no grownups,
Just a chance to kick back and be alright.
I just need some pizza and doughnuts.
It's a little weeknight bonus.
Tuesday's little delight.
I put up my "Keep Out" sign to stay focused,
And so my 'rents will know to keep out of site.
Tonight my room is not open.
I'm chillin' with "Me" tonight.

Macaroni Was My Goldfish

I really wanted a cute little puppy,
But my Mom got me a goldfish instead.
His face looked kind of grumpy,
But I could put him right next to my bed.

That little fish was awesome.
He listened to all of my problems.
Macaroni is what I called him.
He helped me through my summer boredom.

I'd watch him swim around in circles.
I would try and pet him with my finger.
I drew pictures of him in my journal.
I could tell he was a thinker.

I knew it would happen eventually,
I just didn't think it would be tonight.
I thought he would live forever, potentially.
But my little goldfish Macaroni, well, he died.

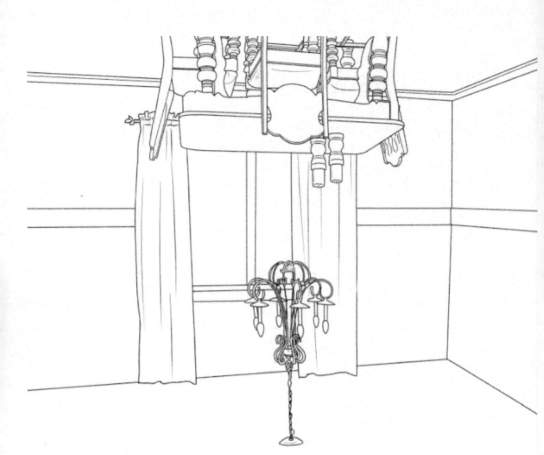

My Downright, Upbeat, Imaginary World

I often think when I'm daydreaming at night,
Of a place in a space where nothing is right.

All of the rooms everywhere are flipped upside down.
When you're walking on the ceiling, it's actually the ground.

Your dining room table, candles, and chairs are up above.
You're walking around the chandelier that is sticking straight up.

It doesn't make sense, but what makes sense these days?
I think about how I'd walk around there, go to bed, or play.

My Mom said, "You know things like that cannot be real".
I said, "If Thomas Edison's mom said that, there wouldn't be light in here".

Peter's Funny Bone

His dog wanted a bone,
So Peter gave him what he had.
Rover laughed so hard he moaned.
Peter tried to laugh right back.

Peter couldn't laugh until his dog brought it over.
It was his funny bone he accidentally gave to Rover.

Paper Chain of Impatience

My teacher has this paper chain, for a countdown to the holidays.
Every morning she tears off a link to show how far we are away.

At first, the holidays seemed to be pretty close.
Maybe this paper chain represents my impatience, who knows.

By the time the holidays get here, I'll probably be 20 years old.
"One more day away," my teacher says, as my eyes begin to roll.

A constant reminder, hanging from up high,
That the days before the holidays, won't be flying by.

Check Yes?

I wanted to know if she liked me, so I did what you're supposed to do.
I wrote a note, passed it back, and waited patiently for it to get through.

I told her to check yes or no, to see if she liked me back.
My anxiety was building as it made its way to the back of class.

It was almost there and I was excited to see her face.
I hoped she would say yes, because my heart had started to race.

Just when I thought I couldn't wait one second more,
It had reached her desk, but she got up and walked out the door.

My note just sat there, while she went to the restroom.
I hoped that she would come back into class real soon.

There was my note, just back there getting cold.
I was just patiently waiting for my future to be told.

Little Letters

I write letters to myself,
As little reminders.
I put them up on my shelf,
And sometimes in my binder.

I remind myself of a lot of things,
Like "be kind" and "push through".
"Let the world pull on your heart strings."
"Do that thing that you wanted to do!"

I tell myself to be nicer to my sister.
I remind myself I want to eat cake soon.
I tell myself to be a better listener.
I tell myself to remember that new tune.

I tell myself to laugh more.
I write down funny things.
I also write down my chores.
It makes my Mom happy.

Little notes to my future self,
Placed in my later vision.
It really does help,
In making my daily decisions.

The Little Fish and His Big Dream

The little fish in the great big stream,
Swam so fast, chasing his dream.

Charging and dodging every obstacle,
He felt alive, he felt irresponsible.

As fast as he could, swim swim swim.
The water was getting a little too dim.

Then he saw it and what a delight!
An area he had heard of with no other fish in sight.

He sat in that spot and basked in all its glory.
He kicked his fin up and read a story.

He put his fins behind his head,
And thought about the kind of life he lived.

He was so very happy to just take a break,
From the fast paced world that is always awake.

After some hours he made his way back,
A slow-paced fish on a slow-paced track.

He was in no hurry to return back to the fuss,
But he made plans later with an Octopus.

He swam peacefully, knowing he'd be back there soon,
To the place where he felt the beat of his own tune.

This World

Despite what you might think,

This world is in sync.

Don't go off and hide.

The world is on your side.

The world is not trying to throw any attacks.

You just have to love the world and the world will love you back.

My Tree Harold

I'm going to grow a tree in my room and I'm naming him Harold.
His trunk will be dark brown and his leaves will look like emeralds.

I'll put my bed by the trunk and hang my things on his branches.
I won't ever, EVER light candles. I don't want to take any chances.

I'll swing around on him and climb to the very top.
I'll ask him how his day is and offer him a soda pop.

We will laugh and he'll say, "I'll just take a splash of water".
I hope that my tree, Harold, will be a talker.

Just me and my tree Harold, being us.
When I leave for school, he'll put up a big fuss.

He will wait around for me and ease my school stress.
I just need to ask my Mom first, but I'm sure she'll say yes.

Sweet Peggy Perry

Sweet, sweet Peggy Perry, always smelled like sweet strawberries!
I thought I knew how once, but it wasn't the lunch she carries.

Her cheeks were so rosy and she was always so kind.
To me that's just how sweet people smelled in my mind.

One day I figured it out when she stood next to me for a picture.
She wears some, well a lot, of scratch and sniff stickers.

Stephen the Shark's Secret

Stephen the shark had a secret.
He no longer wanted to keep it.

He called all the fish from the sea.
He said, "Hey guys, come listen to me."
They all did so reluctantly.

He said, "This may not seem cliché,
But I'm a shark who loves to crotchet."

All the fish laughed about how funny it was,
So in one swoop he had them all in his jaws.

When he spit them out they all stopped laughing.
They said, "That's cool Stephen and we think your scarf is dashing!"

Ready for Bed and Tomorrow

I figured out something great,
And it's extremely convenient.
It saves me time so I'm not late.
If I must say it, it's genius.

Every night before I go to bed,
I get completely dressed for the next day.
Then when I wake up, I'm a little ahead.
Only a few last steps and I'm on my way!

I put on my pants, t-shirt and socks,
Then I tie my robe over it.
I give my parents the goodnight talk.
I tell them goodnight and then split.

Then I go in my room and take off my robe.
This might be my best idea yet.
I get all snuggled up in my next day's clothes,
And sleep worry free under my blanket.

Best Friend Hand Shake

I have a special handshake
With my best friend and it's rad.
It starts out with a quick fake,
Then we elbow tap a tad.

We slowly bump our fists,
Then let them shatter and explode.
We swiftly shake our wrists,
And then we shake them slow.

We start to bend our knees.
We get down really low.
After a real quick freeze,
We start to dance and flow.

Then we go about our day.
Like it never even happened.
We move along going separate ways,
Like it was all just imagined.

I Want to Be Your Sweatpants

I want to be your sweatpants.

I'll keep you comfortable and warm.

When I'm around, you can be yourself.

If I'm not hugging you, I'm there if you need one.

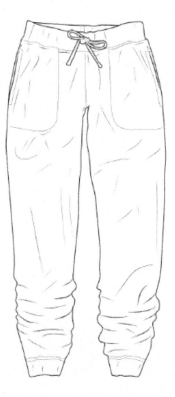

PBJ Huggles

Sometimes, when I hug someone really, really hard,

So hard it feels like we could never be pulled apart,

When we get all hug-cozy because we may be here a while,

And we are both wearing a really big smile,

And it's a snuggle-hug where we use all of our might,

It makes me wonder if that's what peanut butter and jelly feel like.

Zoo Day

I want to go to the Zoo.
I really, really do.
But I want to do it like when I was two.
Where I ride in a stroller and get pushed by you.
You would feed me snacks and tie my shoes.
I would relax and see animals the whole day through.
That's how I want to go to the zoo.
Just kick back and enjoy the view.

Crazy Pants

My favorite thing to do is wear some crazy pants.
I have pants with stripes, polka dots, and some that look weird at first glance.

I have leopard print, zebra print, tiger print and cheetah print.
I have some kind-of-fuzzy ones that always pick up lint.

However, on this particular day, I wanted to do something really strange.
I just wore some plain, normal jeans to try a little change.

Then I stood and looked in the mirror. I was excited but terrified.
That person staring back at me, I barely even recognized.

My Lazy Cat Feisty

I named my cat Feisty, but thinking back now it's silly.

He's the laziest cat there is, he doesn't go anywhere quickly.

He stares out the window, licks his paws and lies around.

He's without a doubt, 100%, the laziest cat in town.

When I call his name, he just looks and turns the other way.

Just so he doesn't have to move, or come over here and play.

He doesn't put up any fuss, just lies around nightly.

I named him a little too early, my lazy cat, Feisty.

Mom Love

I like it when my Mom says that she likes my drawings.

Truth be told, they aren't that great and I probably have another calling.

She just gets so tickled and happy when I show her what I made.

I tell her that I had to do it, so I could get a good grade.

She hangs it up for all to see and is so proud it's on display.

I guess when you love a kid like me so much, you can't see straight.

Cailey and Her Ukulele

Sweet little Cailey,
Loved to play her ukulele.

She played until the day was done.
When she played all the birds would come.

The birds were happy and so carefree,
But they disturbed her poodle Geoffrey.

So she only played when Geoffrey was inside.
Geoffrey was cheery when the birds were out of sight.

Pumpermuffles Loves My Shoes

I don't know if my cat loves me,
But he definitely loves my shoes.
Whenever they are lying around,
It's like I'm old news.

No, this way, I'm over here!
Hello Pumpermuffles, it's me!
Oh, I see you're busy with my shoes.
Well, just let me know when you're free.

Get Out Here Monster

There's a Monster in my closet.
I want to tell him to come on out.
I've got toys and chocolate.
He could see what my room was all about.

I've got a pretty big bed he could sleep under.
I've got movies for a rainy day.
He could keep me safe from the thunder.
I could show him how I do ballet.

"Come hang out closet Monster!
I made tea and it's almost ready.
You're welcome to come and wander.
Pretty please with sprinkles and a cherry?"

I'm Still Wearing the Smile You Gave Me

I just wanted to say thank you, for that smile you gave me earlier.

I was having a bad day and you came by, like a little happiness courier.

It brightened me up my whole day through, like a little beam of glee.

It's evening now, and I'm still wearing that smile that you gave me.

Instant Best Friends

It happened last Tuesday exactly.
It was about twelve o'clock.
My lunch was satisfactory.
Peanut Butter and jelly wasn't a shock.

Then another girl came and sat at my table.
She had puppies on her lunch box.
She had ham and cheese on a bagel.
She said she liked my socks.

Anyone who likes silly sock attire,
Is really cool in my book.
She offered me half of that sandwich I admired.
I gave her some mac and cheese my Mom cooked.

We laughed and played all during recess.
It was the best time I've ever had.
I'd say Tuesday was quite a success.
I made a new best friend and I was glad.

It's crazy how it happened so fast.
We've been best friends ever since.
It has been SUCH a blast,
As we go through our daily events.

She gives me compliments all day,
When I'm sometimes feeling sad.
"You're the best," I'll say.
"You're the greatest," she'll add.

Grounded

I got grounded for a week because I ate a box of cereal at midnight.
It's been really, super hard, but I guess I'm doing alright.

It gets lonely sometimes and can be so incredibly boring.
I basically just sit around and listen to my dad on the couch snoring.

I get it, I did the crime and I'm learning my lesson.
It's just that I have an uncontrollable sugar obsession.

But through all this tough time I've learned to handle it.
I walk around, stand, walk around again and then sit.

All this hard time has really helped and I think you'll agree.
Only six more days and 23 hours of grounding left for me.

Silly Billy

Silly Billy was full of laughter.
He always acted first and thought after.

He kept getting older, but wore the same clothes.
If there was a choice, it was fun that he chose.

He had such a good sense of humor.
He grew taller, but was a late bloomer.

His life was telling him to act his age.
It wanted to go to the next chapter, but Billy wouldn't turn the page.

My Dog's Head Tilt

My dog tilts his head at me and it drives me insane.
I'm thankful for my dog George, so it's hard to complain.
It's just that, I feel like he usually just gets me,
So when he tilts his head, I think, "How can this be?"
I'm like George, it's me, we go way back.
Look at you, all you want is a snack.
Are you even listening or are you really confused?
Hello, it's me Keegan, why aren't you enthused?
Really, a head tilt, what don't you get?
You're at home, it's normal, so that's not it.
Do you want something like a TOY?
I think a TREAT might be something you'd enjoy!
You're so adorable, go on and tilt your head.
But I did say TREAT, did you hear what I said?

Hey Ocean!

I stood at the ocean for the very first time.

I splashed around, I had some fun, and I was feeling fine.

The water kept coming and coming in a waving motion.

At first it was a little scary, but I thought, "What a silly ocean."

I looked at the next wave and as I saw it come,

I said, "Hey Ocean, wave if you think I'm awesome!"

What's so Great?

When I figure it out, I'll let everyone know.
I'm sure I'll figure it out as I go.

It has to be something powerful and strong,
Whatever is so great in this world that we can't get along.

It probably has the power of everyone's muscles combined,
Along with some kind of mega-mind.

I wonder if it's a monster and if so, is it green?
Maybe a monster scary enough to make adults scream.

We should all be so right, so why are we so wrong?
What is so great in this world that we can't get along?

Snow Day

I watched for the updates and paced across the room.
If they say my school, I'm putting on my snow day costume.

Every snow day, I wear my pajamas (they're tiger print).
"Did he say Brown Elementary?" I thought he did but he didn't.

Come on weather man, it's snowing so much outside!
I'm ready to curl up with some hot chocolate by my side.

If he doesn't say my school, I'm going to cry.
I can kiss this really fun Monday goodbye.

He finished the school list and didn't say it.
Why is our school the only one that's not on the list?

I walked out and I stomped as hard as I could.
I threw a fit and it wasn't good.

I asked my cat, "What are you looking at Fluffy?!
You get to sit around and get real comfy."

I had given up and was about to change the channel.
Then the announcer said, "Brown Elementary is also cancelled."

I cheered and cheered and then apologized to my cat.
A snow day, a snow day, it'll be just that!

One Day You'll Realize

One day you'll realize that I'm one of a kind.

You'll realize people like me are hard to find.

Soon you'll realize I have such a big heart.

You'll know that I was there for you from the start.

If you're looking around, wondering where I could be.

I'll be with the people who appreciate me.

My Room

This is the room I live in.
I've got clothes, a bed, and a toy bin.
I've got cartoon posters on my wall,
And a little hoop with a foam basketball.
I've got some shoes. I've got some books.
I've got all my jackets on their jacket hooks.
This is the room I live in.
About eight years it's been.
I've got all the things I need.
I'm pretty sure my Mom agrees.
All of the world's happenings
Can sometimes get challenging.
I'm just a growing boy with himself to show.
The rest of the world, I don't know.
But this is the room I live in.
I just sit in here and grin.
Until my Mom asks if I'm hungry,
Then I leave this room in a scurry.

Breakfast for Dinner

I want to eat breakfast for dinner and dinner for breakfast.

Everyone is putting up a fuss, like I'm doing something reckless.

Why are there rules in place on what to eat and when?

Maybe I'd like a hot dinner meal in the morning, every now and then.

For dinner, sometimes cereal or pancakes sound marvelous!

I'm just going to eat what I want, it doesn't seem too harmless.

Maybe I'm getting wild.

Maybe my mind is scattered.

Maybe I'm just a child,

Who likes to break the pattern.

Kiwi's Nest

Kiwi was a sweet little bird,
Who wanted to make herself a nest.
She transferred sticks to a tree in the yard,
Because that's what she thought would work best.

She would make this tree her home base.
She spent all day weaving sticks together.
She wanted to create a good tidy place,
So she could have visitors like her sister and mother.

When she was almost finished building,
Along came a big gust of wind.
Her work seemed so unfulfilling,
After the breeze put her nest in a spin.

Kiwi realized it was going to be a long day,
But she went back to building again.
She hoped that the wind stayed away,
She had plans later with a crow named Madeline.

This Old Man

This nice old man once told me, you can be whatever you want to be.
I asked if I could be a bird and he said yes, that it was all up to me.
I asked if I could be a tree, a Martian, a bug or someone who just eats ice cream.
He said yes, yes, yes, you can be anything you want to be.
I told him I didn't understand and asked if he could please explain it to me.
He said you control your actions and thoughts and wants and dreams.
I said I want to be a fish and swim through every river and stream.
He said don't concentrate on other things, I am me and you are you.
Think about all the things that a little person like you can do.
So I thought and thought and thought, then told him I didn't know.
He said to follow my heart and thoughts, and they'll show me where to go.
The one last thing he said was to listen to yourself first.
In your head there is a land where all your dreams will burst.
I don't understand it all, but I do know that one day I will.
To take on this world with my heart and dreams, is going to be quite the thrill.
So don't forget what this nice man told me once, I'm passing it to you.
Be whatever you want to be and do what you want to do.

Support-O-Posse

Some days I just need some cool people around

To pat me on my back and have a laugh when I'm down.

I'd tell them they're awesome they would tell me I'm kind.

I would say they are incredible, they'd say I had a beautiful mind.

And it would carry on and carry on, for hours in the day,

Because sometimes you just need some support along the way.

Love, joy and good friends are the things that aren't too costly.

Keep those things around you, to create a Support-O-Posse!

Bewildered Delight

Let us get lost in this great big world.

Let us be in the air of wishing swirls.

Let us appreciate the hope in this place.

Let us drift towards a friendly face.

Let us not get settled in normal ways.

Let us spark a wishful blaze.

Let our emotions take flight.

Let us get baffled by all the sites.

Let us know that we can change things.

Contentment might be the enemy.

Let us understand when things aren't quite right.

Then, let us get lost in bewildered delight.

Your Inner Sparkles

You are born with inner sparkles,
Like glitter sprinkled in your soul.
Your eyes have twinkling particles.
Don't ever let them get dull.

Keep the light in your eyes.
Get lost in a daydream.
Love each day's surprise.
Let your inner light beam.

Look at yourself, you are fabulous.
Don't ever, ever lose it.
Those little beats of happiness
Or the sparkles in your spirit.

Sometimes we get lost
In the wish-wash of the grey.
So be the brightest color,
Your OWN color every day.

Confetti Time

It's normal to throw confetti,
At a time when everyone's ready.

I wait until nobody knows I have it.
For random good news, I keep it in my jacket.

I throw it at just the right time.
When they don't see it coming, it blows their minds.

Who Is on the Telephone?

Who is on the telephone?
Is it a witch, a puppy or a friend at home?

Oh, I wish I could call whomever.
I'd call my dog, spaghetti, or my friend Trevor.

I would tell everyone my thoughts and dreams
On that little phone that talks and rings.

I would tell them about the lamp I named Steve,
Or how I rode my bike and watched TV.

Maybe I'd even tell whomever, where I hid my secret treasure.
No that's a secret I'll keep forever...
Ok, it's under my dresser.

Oh please just let me make one phone call.
It'll just take 5 minutes and I'll be in the hall.

I'd call the tooth fairy and a lot of reindeer.
I'd call everyone in this hemisphere!

I would say, "Hey, come play, get over here!"
Then I'd play hide and seek and disappear.

Where did he go? Do you think he's near?
Then I'd say HERE I AM, and EVERYONE would cheer!

What's that Mom? You say I need everyone's phone number?
Well, now I'm pretty tired. I think I'll just go slumber.

Paper Airplane

I made a paper airplane.
I imagined I was inside.
I had no time to explain.
I was suddenly in mid-flight.

My room looked so cool from up there.
I stayed far away from the floor.
I dipped, dove, and drifted everywhere.
Woo, I could soar!

I flew all around.
My thoughts were excited.
Even after I came back down,
My imagination was so delighted.

NOT READY TO GROW

SO YESTERDAY WAS MY BIRTHDAY. AND DON'T GET ME WRONG.

I LIKED THE PRESENTS. CAKE AND WHEN EVERYONE SANG THE HAPPY BIRTHDAY SONG.

IT'S JUST THAT I'M NOT READY TO GROW UP TALL AND GET OLD.

I WANT TO BE A KID FOREVER AND I KNOW THAT SOUNDS BOLD.

BUT I JUST GROW AND GROW AND GROW. EVERY DAY DAY DAY.

I KEEP GETTING SO TALL TALL TALL AS I PLAY PLAY PLAY.

I MUST LET YOU GO NOW: I NEED TO MAKE A STAY-YOUNG PLAN.

IF IT DOESN'T WORK YOU CAN FIND ME LATER. I'LL BE THE REALLY OLD TALL MAN.

Innovators

Without innovators, big and small,

I'd just be sitting here, staring at the wall.

There wouldn't be a TV, a computer, or video games.

There wouldn't be pictures or picture frames.

I guess I wouldn't even have a chair,

But I mean, I could sit anywhere.

I would just sit here sta... oh I guess there wouldn't be a wall.

I guess there really wouldn't be anything...at all.

The Clouds

I like to lay and think as I stare up at the clouds,

Alone in the grass and away from any crowds.

I look up and wonder what it would be like to touch them.

If I had something to climb on, a ladder or a long plant stem.

I pick out the images and all the shapes that they make.

I pick out new shapes as the clouds grow and break.

It's a slow-paced game when you need to kick back.

I turn on my imagination to find a car, bird or yak.

Sometimes my Mom checks on me, just a little peep.

Because the last time I did this, I accidently fell asleep.

Tommy Liked to Help

Tommy liked to help people out a lot.

He liked it as much as he liked cheesy tater tots.

He helped his friend Jimmy clean his room.

He helped Susan garden, so her flowers would bloom.

Susan was so pleased, she wanted to make him lunch.

She said, "I can make you a sandwich. Thanks a bunch!"

Tommy told her that helping out was just his language.

He didn't need lunch, but still accepted her gratitude sandwich.

Dreams You Say?

What are these things that take over my head at night?
Something is going on up there while I'm sleeping tight.

It's not always the same and sometimes it gets weird.
Last night I was at school and my Mom was there with a beard.

I know you say they are dreams, but I need you to explain,
The other night I was eating cotton candy and flying an airplane.

You say there is a normal world that I live in each day.
Then there is an imaginary world, where anything takes place?

If I could go into my head during one of these crazy dreams,
I'd say, "HELLO, I'm here to play", and they would all greet me!

They'd say, "We've got a lot for you to see."
I'd sit and eat pizza and watch all the crazy things!
 "Hey you guys, don't you think I should have some wings?"

I don't know what they would say, but it wouldn't hurt to ask.
If I ever get to go in there, I'm sure it'd be a blast.

Noodles

I'd like to see what would happen, if everyone's legs turned to noodles.
I know what it would look like (I've drawn lots of doodles).

I feel like we'd be shaking and grooving and laughing.
I'd say, "Well hey everyone, you all look quite dashing."

We'd wiggle around and of course we'd all have smiles.
It would be a wiggle town, with wigglers wiggling for miles!

Maybe it would just be once a week, probably on Saturdays.
Saturday is the day when everyone wiggle-waggles and sways.

It would be a day for zigzagging with friends and family.
People would do their normal routine but jiggle around happily.

One day I'll be a crazy scientist and then I'll see what I can do.
Right now I'll take my normal legs downstairs to get some food.
Spaghetti sounds good for some reason...

Lazy

I just realized I can do what I want,
But now I'm just plain lazy.
My inner voices can taunt and taunt,
But now I just do what I want and it's crazy.

They are saying I have to clean,
But really, really, do I?
The grown-ups may be mean,
But just relaxing is worth a try.

It does, this feels real nice.
I really will get up later.
I will probably pay the price,
But this feels a lot better.

Create Your Own World

You can create your own world in your head you know.

You can add different things as you go.

You can paint in colors we have yet to see.

You can be anything you want to be.

You can create, start over and create again.

And if there is something spectacular within,

Maybe you could bring it out and share.

For there's a world out here too, that can look a little bare.

The Ice Cream Frenzy

I stormed through the hall in quite the frenzy.

I hoped my piggy bank wasn't out of money.

I got in my room and scurried through my closet.

I emptied my piggy bank and my pant pockets.

When I got back up, I tripped over clothes but was okay.

I thought, "Please, oh please, ice cream truck, don't go away!"

I thought I still heard the tune, but it was getting quieter.

I should really run around more, so I don't get so tired.

I opened the door and to my own horror,

I saw the ice cream truck, but it just turned the corner.

My Belongings

My belongings are cool.

My belongings are neat.

I've got toys, a golden stool,

And tricky games I can sometimes beat.

I've got stuffed animals.

One of them looks like a camel.

I enjoy each and every one,

But when it's all said and done,

I just like things that you can't touch.

Those are the things I love so much.

Like hope, joy, love, and happy thoughts.

I like to keep those in special spots.

All of those things that I truly treasure,

Are things that you are unable to measure.

I keep those things on a secret shelf,

One that I keep deep down inside of myself.

Ba dum Ba dum

Ba dum ba dum
I'm here for you.
Ba dum ba dum
Your guidance of truth.

Ba dum ba dum
Just listen my dear.
Ba dum ba dum
I'll help you conquer fears.

Ba dum ba dum
I'll be your guiding light.
Ba dum ba dum
You'll be alright.

Ba dum ba dum
I'm your heart.
Ba dum ba dum
I'm where your dreams start.

Ba dum ba dum
Listen close.
Ba dum ba dum
You're scared I know.

Ba dum ba dum
Just follow me.
Ba dum ba dum
I'll help you be.

Ba dum ba dum

Ba dum ba dum

Ba dum ba dum

Ba dum ba dum

HEY, STAR...

You look like a bright star.

It's me Sarah. Wow, you're really far.

I just have this little bitty wish.

I don't even know how to do this.

But if you are the star I wish upon,

I wish for happiness before it's all gone.

For every person in every home,

From the tall giraffes to the little gnomes,

Grandmas and grandpas and little bitty babies,

The fish in the ocean and the fields full of daisies.

I want the world to be happy, is it too much to ask?

I know that it's a pretty big task.

I think you're cool, little bright star.

I hope you can hear me, from down this far.

In the Teeth Business

Something crazy happened to me last week.
My tooth started wiggling in my cheek!

My Mom said that it was loose,
I'd lose it and grow another tooth!

That's wild, what a crazy Mom.
She said it wouldn't be long.

Then it came out while I was eating!
I almost started screaming.

Then my Mom said something strange,
"A tooth fairy will come for it and leave you change."

I was amazed, but shocked.
Would the tooth fairy even knock?

In the morning, quarters were under my pillow!
The tooth fairy was gone; I even looked out the window.

Then I got a crazy thought
I'd collect teeth, sell them to her and make a lot.

I'd set up in my yard with one of those big stands.
"Hey, need to get those old teeth off your hands?"

It turns out that old teeth are hard to come by.
People don't give them up. I guess I can see why.

Mr. Happy

They call him Mr. Happy and I'd say rightfully so.

He's been smiling ever since a long time ago.

A brave kid once asked him if he thought he could be happy forever.

He said that since he has made up his mind to, his life has been so much better.

He kept on smiling and laughing. It was quite a sight to see.

A man that just chose to be happy and is as happy as can be.

I Wonder

There are a lot of things I wonder about, when I get lost in my thoughts.
When I think about them too much, my brain gets into knots.

I think about who said night was night and day was day.
What if we slept in the day and at night we could play?

Who thought that grass would be the best thing for a yard?
I think that a bouncy ground would be the best by far.

If they can make strawberry, chocolate and vanilla into Neapolitan ice cream,
Can't they make a bed that makes itself, so I'll have longer to dream?

I like my dog and all, but why are just some animals our pets?
I'd like to take care of a little panda. I would even take it to the vet.

These are some things I wonder, when I get all up in my head.
Then I have some crazy dreams whenever I go to bed.

Jane

Jane loved to slide down the stairs.

She said that she wasn't even scared.

She didn't give a reason why she didn't do it anymore.

She just said there were other things she would rather explore.

Hopeful

It's funny how hope squeezes through.
It works its way down deep inside of you.
It plants itself inside of your thoughts,
Then grows and grows and grows a lot.
Give hope the things that it needs.
Then follow it to see where it leads.
When you start to wonder how it got there in the first place...
Stop.

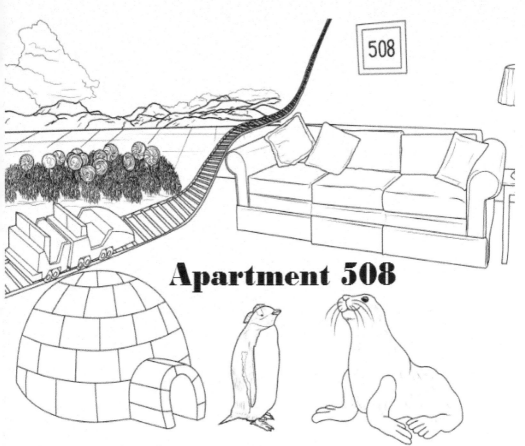

Apartment 508

There is quite a story about apartment 508.
It's a secret land that everyone inside creates.

Whenever you enter it, it takes things from your imagination.
It stirs up everyone's minds and makes some cool creations!

I heard about a group of 12 kids who all went inside together.
They created mountains, clouds you can eat, and some sunny weather.

The floor jiggled and you could bounce all around on it.
There were all sorts of light bulbs in the light sockets.

There were twirling lollipops and a penguin with a squawk.
They could all do belly flops and the penguin could talk.

There was a rollercoaster that took them all to Mars and back before dinner.
There was an igloo they could go inside, but they couldn't help but shiver.

The kids laughed and played and imagined all day long.
It was a place they made up and a place they all belonged.

So if you see an apartment that is labeled 508,
It could be the very one. What would your mind create?

Making Music

Give me all the music makers of every shape and size.
Drums, thumbs, some lazy bums and some instruments in disguise.

Bring a sax, some quacks and symbol stacks, all kinds of noise makers.
You don't need anything fancy, just bring along some shakers.

So get hoppin', boppin' and choppin', it's time to create.
Just come along, bring something to play, and it all will be great.

Noise is just noise, but with some good feelings and soul,
You've got some sweet songs, fun music, and it's time to rock and roll.

Your music becomes messages for the entire world to discover.
So come along all you music makers, let's make some tuneful thunder.

Don't Forget to Look

Don't forget to look when you open your eyes.
It's tricky when they're open but sometimes disguised.
You see things around you, but don't actually look.
Look into the depths of things, in every space and nook.

Don't forget to listen, when sounds go in your ear.
Don't get so busy, that the sounds disappear.
Listen to the words, the music, and the air.
Don't think too hard about other things, that you forget to care.

Don't forget to feel, what you can touch and what you cannot.
We are pretty clever beings and we are able to feel a lot.
Sometimes life can get tricky and you forget the important things,
So don't forget to look around and see what the world brings.

Limitless

People say the sky is the limit.

I say that's not true.

That would mean that sky inhibits,

The things that you want to do.

Aim far, aim wide, aim high.

Don't think about boundaries.

Don't ask what, how or why.

Go beyond your surroundings.

Be Nice

Be nice to people, each and every one.

Be kind to people, it really is fun.

Help people and go out of your way.

Smile at people each and every day.

Lend an ear to those who need a chat.

Lend your strength to those who need just that.

When you find yourself at a place where you're the one in need,

Reach out to people and they may offer you a good deed.

If you learn that it is the people in your life that you should treasure,

It will be the people in your life that make living so much better.

My Little Bearrry Bear

I still carry around my stuffed animal, it's true.

It weird, but I have done it since I was two.

It doesn't have one of its eyes anymore.

His fuzzy fur has gotten quite worn.

He's my buddy, through thick and thin.

He reminds me how far I've been.

My little Beary Bearrry Bear.

Don't listen to my mom, you're not going anywhere.

Don't Give a Worry

Don't give a worry and don't let things dwell.

Save your mind for wonders, because worries are bad spells.

Worries take up space in your mind that could be used for something else,

Like a hope, a thought, or wonderment, so be good to yourself.

Don't fill your mind with things you cannot change right now.

Use your mind to lift your spirits while the world figures things out.

Then come back to it later, once you've had a little space.

You'll know better then, when your mind is in a better place.

Silence in My Ears

It's weird how the quiet makes my ears feel alive.
They tingle at the sound of nothing.
They are excitedly waiting for a sound to arrive.
Even the silence seems like it's buzzing.

I can hear the cool night air come rushing.
My ears listen as it comes all around.
The goose bumps are quickly overcoming,
As they listen in the silence for a sound.

I Dress Myself on Fridays

I have this deal with my Mom and I get to dress myself on Fridays.
I can wear whatever I want, like crazy pants or my hat sideways.

I could wear two shirts, one sneaker and one flip-flop.
I could wear random things like pants with shorts on top.

I wanted to wear jeans and a plain shirt, it's pretty normal I'd say.
I chose it because that is what I wanted to wear today.

Perhaps in the future, I will put together some crazy outfits.
Today it's just a regular old thing, but it's better because I picked it.

I Color

I color inside the lines.

I color outside the lines.

I color everything in my mind.

I add my own designs.

I always take my time.

I watch it all intertwine.

I do it until it looks like mine.

Use Your Words

Use your words. They're what you've got.

If you keep them inside, they settle and rot.

Speak about your feelings, wishes, and dreams,

When they're released, they send out a word stream.

Into this great big world is where your words will go.

Give them to the world so that the world knows.

Maybe they'll be heard and maybe they'll inspire.

Maybe you'll be answered, maybe you'll be admired.

Your words may go through many people and places as they swirl in the air,

But if you keep them all inside of you, they won't be able to go anywhere.

My Lamp Winston

I named my lamp Winston one day,
And now I feel like he's real.
I know that it seems like child's play,
But now I always wonder how he feels.

I greet him every time I come in.
He must get really bored.
I'm sure he wonders where I've been
And all the territory I've explored.

Maybe I'll bring him around with me.
No I won't, I know that he's not real.
Maybe just go outside so he can see.
Winston is going to think it's unreal!

Lily the Chihuahua

Lily was a Chihuahua who barked a lot.

She was a protector, or so she thought.

She would yap yap yap all day long.

When nothing was near, she was mean and strong.

When something came around, then she would go and hide.

She once saw a leaf blow by and she was terrified.

Dreamer

They call me ridiculous, but I'm a dreamer.
I've got a lot of weird things on my agenda.
I'm overheated with an explorer's fever.
I'll paint this dull world with turquoise and magenta.

They say I'm going nowhere, but I'm going somewhere different.
I've got some things to get into.
I'm using my creativity to produce something brilliant.
Not everything is see-through.

They call me ridiculous, but I'm a dreamer.

The Ocean?

I often wonder, what's going on in the ocean?
It's so big and always greeting me with a waving motion.

I think I'd like to go and explore it,
Swim around and meet the fish for a bit.

I think I'd like to meet a whale
And ask if I could do flips off his tail!

I'd hold on to a tentacle of an octopus.
Don't worry Mom, I'll be cautious.

I would high five a sting ray.
The ocean would know I was there to play.

I'd play hide and seek in the seaweed.
A good time seems guaranteed.

I would take pictures of the little starfish,
Or I would paint them, I'm quite the artist.

I'd search around for buried treasure.
I feel like I could do that forever!

I'd have a special signal, like a big light that would shine,
That my mom would send me, when it's dinner time.

Because after a day of swimming, I know I'll be ready,
For a really big plate of my mom's famous spaghetti!

Bedtime Stories

I love a good bedtime story.
I read it with all its glory.
I get snuggled up real tight,
For a journey before I go to sleep at night.
It could take me to a beach or a forest,
Or a far away land with a Tyrannosaurus.
One is about a cow named Blue.
He liked to sing instead of moo.
For tonight, I'm still trying to decide.
The adventures are spread far and wide.
Tonight I picked one about a kid like me.
A kid who can be anything he wants to be.
One day I'll write a story about myself.
All the kids will have it on their shelf.
They would love it and I would beam.
They would have adventures with me in their dreams.
Bedtime stories are my favorite thing.
I better get to writing.

Markel

Never sneak up on sweet little Markel.
One small noise and she gets so startled.

She has always been a little skittish.
Scary movies she'll never finish.

When I'm around she thinks, "Oh, geez."
She always gets so startled when I sneeze.

My Stuffed Closet

In my closet I dared to go.

How it got so messy? I don't know.

I opened the door and couldn't see in.

Oh, that is where my pillow has been.

Lots of things without space between,

But at least the rest of my room was clean.

Goodnight y'all, dream big.

CPSIA information can be obtained at www.ICGtesting.com
Printed in the USA
LVOW04s0920041015

456839LV00019B/814/P